Hopes and dreams had grown and died. Spells and magic had filled the castle with a million ghosts and demons as the alchemists had sunk deeper and deeper into witchcraft. The people grew poor and their lives grew bleak and dark as their taxes were wasted on the alchemists' quests for gold.

But it had all come to nothing.

Spinifex was the nineteenth alchemist. He was grasping and secretive and mistrusted everyone, especially his young apprentice, Arthur.

In the great library, thousands of books recorded all the old experiments. Spinifex searched through them for clues, and in his laboratory he constructed fantastic new experiments.

But they all came to nothing.

The king was running out of
patience. He knew that if his
alchemist could create gold, it
would make him the greatest
king who had ever lived.

"If you can make gold by the
Millennium, I will heap riches
and glory upon you," said the
king. "But if you fail me, Spinifex,
you're finished."

As the weeks passed, the alchemist grew more and more anxious. He ransacked the great library again and again, destroying the ancient books in his anger.

"We need more gold," said Spinifex, "to act as a catalyst."

He sent Arthur out to search, and the boy found gold everywhere. Sunshine, canaries, marigolds, egg yolks—a thousand and one things that shone like gold.

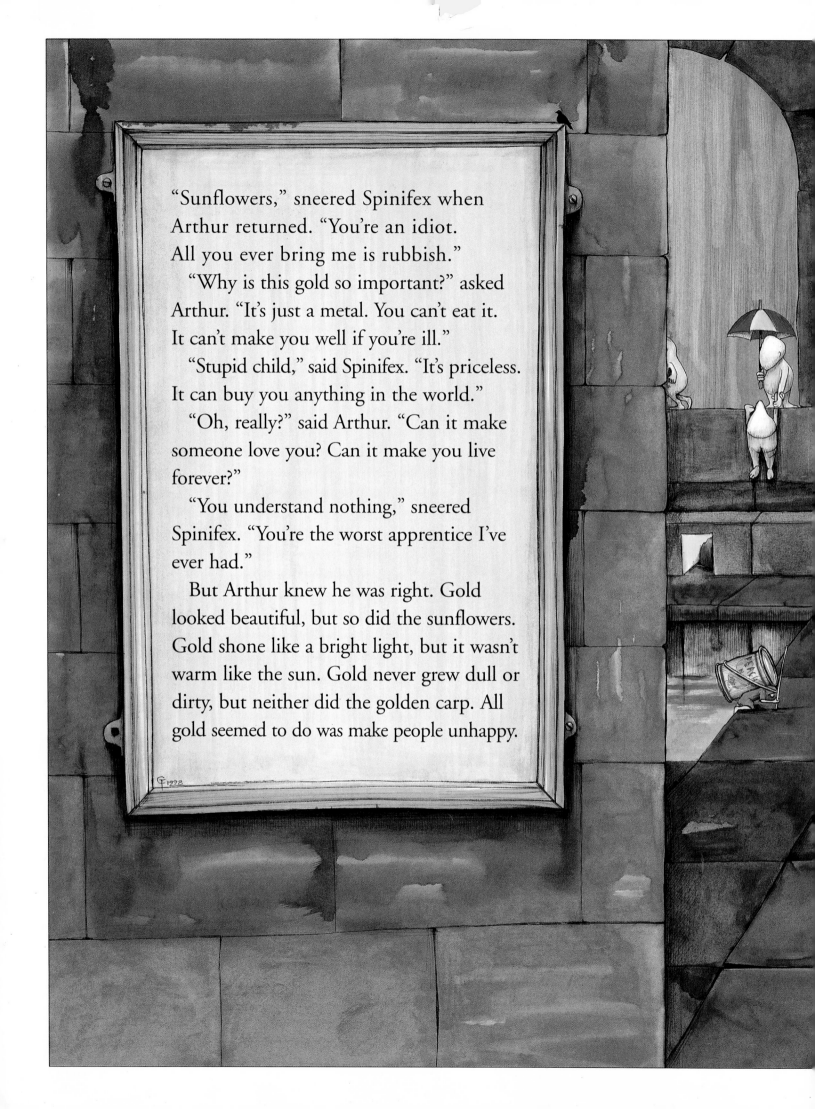

"Sunflowers," sneered Spinifex when Arthur returned. "You're an idiot. All you ever bring me is rubbish."

"Why is this gold so important?" asked Arthur. "It's just a metal. You can't eat it. It can't make you well if you're ill."

"Stupid child," said Spinifex. "It's priceless. It can buy you anything in the world."

"Oh, really?" said Arthur. "Can it make someone love you? Can it make you live forever?"

"You understand nothing," sneered Spinifex. "You're the worst apprentice I've ever had."

But Arthur knew he was right. Gold looked beautiful, but so did the sunflowers. Gold shone like a bright light, but it wasn't warm like the sun. Gold never grew dull or dirty, but neither did the golden carp. All gold seemed to do was make people unhappy.

So Spinifex went out to look for more gold himself. He traveled to every corner of the country, from the great mountains that ringed three sides of their land to the southern plains that rolled into the sea. In the name of the king he took everyone's gold, their goblets and plates, their coins and pendants. He sat by the road prying out the diamonds and the rubies. He even tore the rings from people's fingers.

But all the gold he collected couldn't help him produce more gold. For every ounce of gold he put into an experiment, he got exactly one ounce back.

The weeks passed. The Millennium was only months away. Spinifex grew more and more reckless. His experiments grew wilder and wilder, filling ten rooms at a time. He became more secretive, staying awake for days on end.

Arthur kept out of his way.
From the high gallery, he
watched the crazy old man
run backward and forward
talking to himself a million
words a minute.

Up in the kitchens, Spinifex was the laughingstock of the castle.

"He'll never succeed," said the cook. "Better alchemists than he have tried."

"The only true gold is what's in your heart," said Amy, the cook's daughter.

"I told him that," said Arthur. "But he wouldn't listen."

The weeks passed. The Millennium was now only days away and Spinifex had become completely mad with his obsession. For twenty-seven days and nights he constructed his last great experiment, the experiment that would finally make gold appear where there had been no gold before.

The great machine spread up from the cellars through the castle to the roof, where a giant telescope stood pointing at the sun. Its awesome heat would power this ultimate machine. Far below, in the deepest dungeon, a great crucible stood ready to collect the gold.

Spinifex went to the king. "Soon," he said, "we will both be rich beyond our wildest dreams."

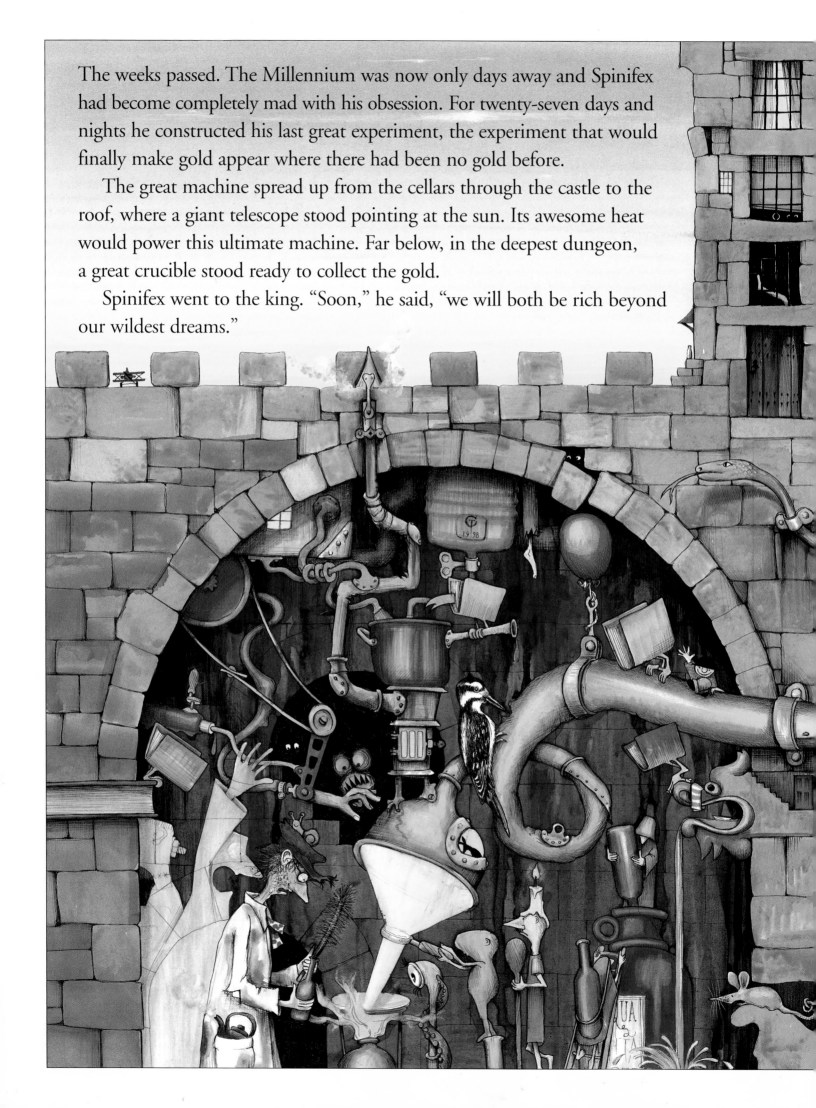

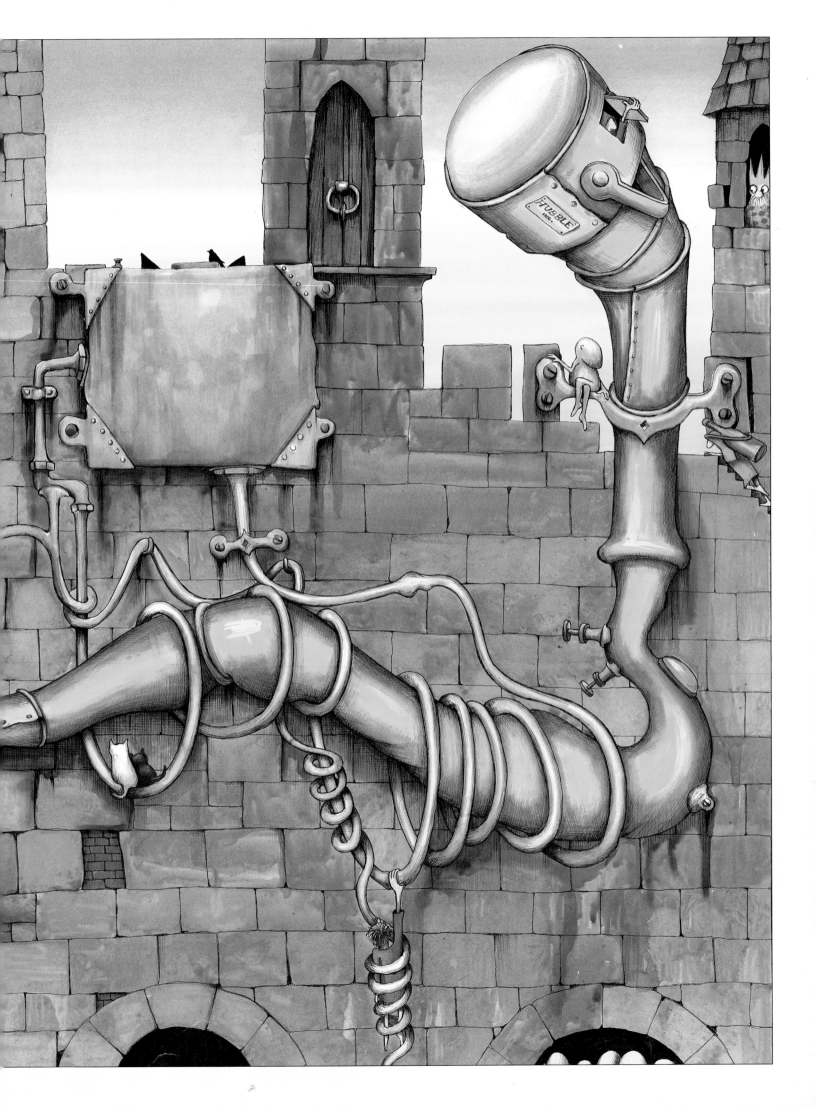

As the sun rose on the first day of the new century, everyone in the castle sat in the high gallery and waited for the miracle. Spinifex pressed the buttons, turned the taps, and slid back the cover. Sunshine poured through the lenses like a great golden waterfall. The heat devoured everything in its path. All the gold that Spinifex had collected was vaporized into the air and settled across the whole country like gleaming mist. Flames shot out in all directions. They caught the alchemist and threw him up into the sky, where he flashed like a starburst and then vanished.

And in the heart of the crucible, all that remained was a tiny pool of brilliant gold.

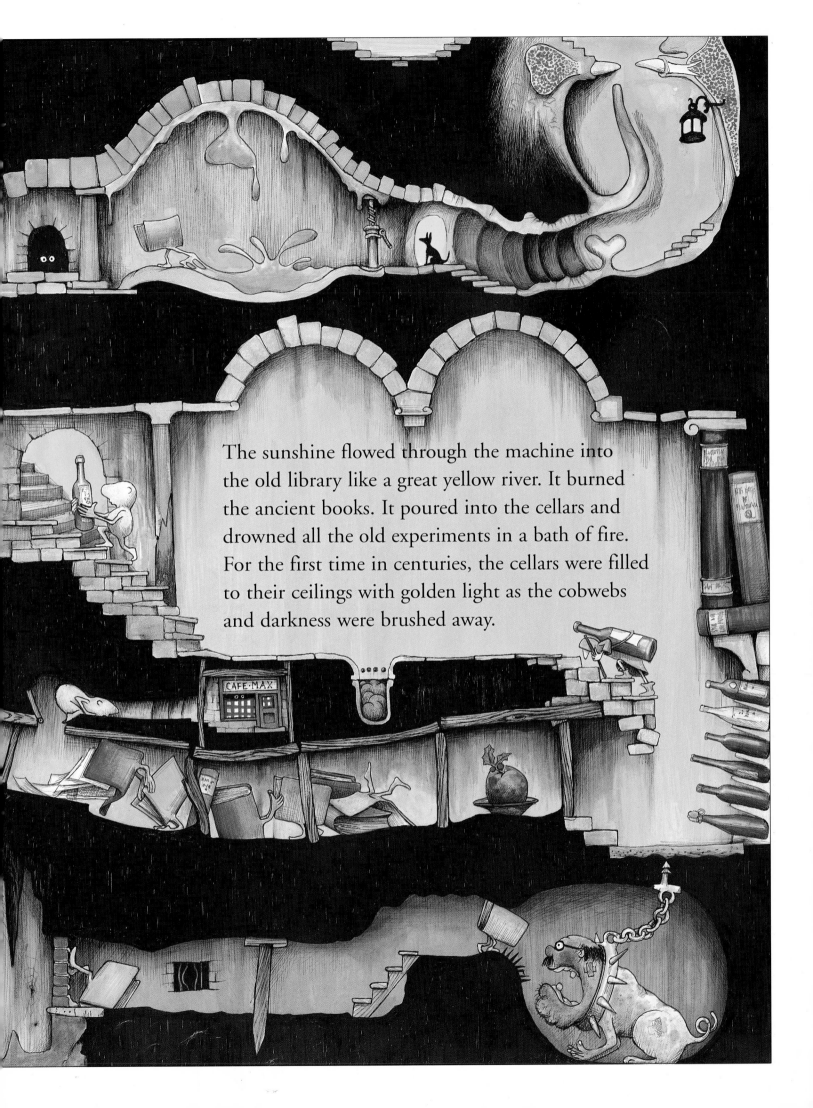

The sunshine flowed through the machine into the old library like a great yellow river. It burned the ancient books. It poured into the cellars and drowned all the old experiments in a bath of fire. For the first time in centuries, the cellars were filled to their ceilings with golden light as the cobwebs and darkness were brushed away.

Arthur took the gold from the crucible and made it into a tiny sunflower for the king. The weeks passed. Spring came and the air grew warm. The winter earth came back to life, fields of sunflowers grew across the southern plains, and everyone felt as if they could live forever.

Even the king came to understand that there were more important things than gold. With the alchemist gone, so were his dreams of wealth. He looked across his kingdom and realized that he had all he could ever want.

One day while he was swimming, the king's tiny sunflower floated away and disappeared into the ocean, where it lay among the coral until the end of time.

Max – 1984-1997

For Anne,
who knows where the real gold is

www.randomhouse.com/kids

Library of Congress Cataloging-in-Publication Data
Thompson, Colin.
The last alchemist / Colin Thompson.
p. cm.
Summary: An alchemist obsessed with making gold finds
that his final experiment has an unexpected result.
ISBN 0-375-80156-1
[1. Alchemy—Fiction. 2. Gold—Fiction.] I. Title.
PZ7.T371424Las
1999
[Fic]—dc21
98-46756

Printed in Singapore
10 9 8 7 6 5 4 3 2 1
First American edition: 1999

Visit Colin Thompson's home page at
www.atlantis.aust.com/~colinet
or e-mail him directly at colinet@atlantis.aust.com